MW01489101

VOLUMES I & II BY JESSE DANIEL EDWARDS

VOLUME I:
SHADOW TIDINGS

VOLUME II:
INSIDE THE BODY IS DARK

jesse daniel edwards

Castoria Publishing House

Typographic design by Andreas Rupert

Manufactured in the United States of America

Published in Canada by Castoria Canada.

Castoria Books are published for the Langston Group by
Castoria Publishing House
New York, NY 10011

Publicity: All Eyes Media Nashville, TN 37213

FIRST PRINTING

for Bonnie

hic requiescet corpus tuum

Table of Contents

xi. Foreword

VOLUME I: SHADOW TIDINGS

pt. I what the sea leaves the sand

1. 6 O'Clock

3. Deep Is Deep

5. Jonny, my earliest of all

6. What Have I Lost

8. The many ways you will feel

9. Tied For Ninth

11. A crop of various tools

13. Take It All

15. Exact me the toll

17. You Are The Accused

19. Requirement Of Innocence

21. Kitchen Session

23. Poor William

24. Remembering To Smile

26. I am the ape

pt. II shapeshifters

28. Your Wilds

30. You, being bound, to a chrysanthemum

33. The Worst Ill

35. Three Tongues Winking Broad

37. Yes, I've been through Unicoi

39. I In Green

41. Silent Game

43. One Tennessean To Another

45. Trading a mother's toy town

46. Dance Or Fight

48. Sing Then Of Ashes

50. I still remember who took that photo

51. Able children of morn

52. Symposium Of Daffodils

pt. III eyelid removal

54. Deserter's Lament

56. Music In The Wind

58. Every Spirit Is Sacred

60. Ask My Desert, Ask The Sun

61. Saint Mark's stitched me up but good

63. All Across Of A Midnight

65. I let go of you the very moment I no longer

67. Just Start Moving

70. Forgetting How To See

72. Behind Us Dark

74. Either way, I'll sleep better tonight

76. Good Dancers

77. You should have seen me, with my petals

79. They got me with the floor plan

VOLUME II: INSIDE THE BODY IS DARK

pt. IV mourn tiger

81. Always so much on the line

82. Hardly Worthy

84. Forget it, Armstrong

86. Wanderlust Companion

88. Aw Men

90. Meadow Queen

92. Upend September

94. Me & Dimitri

97. Two-Handed Saw

99. The Time Of Manu

100. Oh ye host of closet mystics

102. 7 Second Delay

109. King At A Run

pt. V inquisitional soma

111. Dispensation Of Benedictions

113. I can't picture you much other

114. Lost My Birds

116. Take Or Take Leave

118. Filling Space

119. One Of Your Discarded Evenings

121. Exaggerated Cinnabar

123. The Magnetism Of Dust

128. Humorless child...

130. Cherub Tormentor

132. Milk Run, Supposedly

134. Your eyes are almost too tired

136. Bees of Heaven

pt. VI rings around the sun

137. Save The Word Then End It

138. Now do I finally submit

140. I Mainly Squander Daylight

142. Neither Of These

144. So it is

146. Any Every

148. If ever I become a gentle savage

150. In All Her Corners

152. The Beauty Of My Eye's Beholding

154. When I had a reputation

156. Celandines

159. Don't miss this

160. I will plant in the spring

FOREWORD

I have been entreated and entrusted to write the foreword preceding the collection of poems before you. As the "who" behind the "I" hardly matters in this case, think of this account of Jesse Daniel Edwards as scribed from the vantage of a passing *Passer domesticus*.

What universal forces align the orbit of despondent men at cafes and those little brown birds, I cannot say, but I have borne witness to their frenetic scribblings in small notebooks. I've learned by observation and the consumption of errant crumbs that to be a poet is to be a kind of dowser.

They can drink little glasses of 40 year old Port on an Atlantic archipelago, or heavy pours of red table wine somewhere off Rue de Lancry, but they will never be sated. Thus, they follow the rods.

Even in the most inhospitable terrain, they are compelled to find the arcane hiding under sun-choked earth. And when they do finally stumble over an aquifer they will dig until their fingers bleed, for the thirst.

Jesse Daniel Edwards is a poet. In previous iterations of his life, he was a lot of other things too.

Jesse the child of winter born in the sun.
Jesse the first chair wunderkind.
Jesse the street crier.
Jesse the globetrotting rapscallion cad.
Jesse the heartbroken son.

It is one thing to have talent. It is another to be willing to take the chisel to one's own life and meticulously and mercilessly hammer away at it until the true nature of its daemon is revealed.

In one little bird's opinion, this collection is that precise intersection.

In Reverence and with a Wink,
LCNF

Nashville, September 10th, 2024

VOLUME I:
SHADOW TIDINGS

pt. I

what the sea leaves the sand

6 O'Clock

Six o'clock
cannot save me
any
longer,
I do not exist
in the quietude,
but by mid-
night I am
some kind
of animal
again.

I would like
to go back
to Cheboygan,
in the summer,

once before
I can
no longer
...and I will go back
alone. ♦

Deep Is Deep

Still I abide,
by the disgraced rumors
of the heart,
confessionally sewn
into the dawn
of promise.
Don't touch
the wilting refrain
too tenderly,
or risk abandoning
thy pitiful fortune
of honor.
If you are still
carrying each cut,
you are carrying an absence,

of that flesh,
blood,
and bone,
where once they
were not apart.

Deep is
deep enough. ◆

Jonny, my earliest of all,
you are the seed
farmer of my home
town,
I kiss you the most
for your song
of each dayspring,
for adherence
with
out
atonement...

You worked
on
the ground
in
the Air
Force,
I kiss your feet. ♦

What Have I Lost

(Villa Foz Porto Aug 23)

You are not the first
thing I have lost,
or the only
(but perhaps the most dear).
You're made of the same raw bold
raiment, as every other thing else
under sun, that flies 'cross,
end to end, these skies,
but heaven never
had the exact notion
of you.

How I felt
I was possessed

of my secret
me,
with a few wadded up stories,
in a small wooden box,
held within
only a slightly less small
wooden box.

What have I lost,
if not,
the ability to see
in the dark. ✦

(The many ways
you will feel
pain,
only
matched by,
the many ways
you will feel
pleasure.

Think of what
one toe
can do.) ♦

Tied For Ninth

(Berlin Sep 22 for KB)

Me with my,
for instance,
poolside apotheosis,
lining the littlest things
up, by order of priority,
by order of
my borderline authority—
some side
by side,
tied for fourth,
or ninth,
and so on,
still slowly migrating,

from one end
of the bed to
the other,
over the run of night,
ending side
ways,
but having arrived.

I had forgotten you could see me,
so,
I had forgotten the answer to
hello. ♦

A crop of various tools,
for cutting every hole
in the ceiling,
on loan from my gravedigger,
only partially to blame,
there are better sunsets,
with stormier skies,
besides,
whether you do it
good,
or you do it bad,
you do not get it right,
(just ask the upstairs
neighbor, with the lovely
tap dancing machine gun
of a stepwife),

if you get it at all—
which you do not,
the wincing spirit
laid bare,
and left to fry.

Time to pass the wine,
wine to pass the time. ♦

Take It All

(Lapland Helsinki Nov 23)

I have seen better days,
but not in many days,
these modern damned,
ringing out
from swank basement
bomb shelters,
lest someone contest their
sand worn meager pearls,
in excess of petals,
forgiving the apathy
to stay.
I am preparing the way,
for the territorial dispute
of my sad age- come, lord,

I am listening to begin
to arrive,
anonymous,
bearing down,
on the short wave,
blaring from,
the heart land,

I am still bartering
what I did not suffer I owned.

Take it,
take it all. ♦

Exact me the toll,
I pay with what I don't have,
but you would take it,
the ash at long last burns
down to the fingertips,
but longer
than it should
to catch it fly,
and a brisker eternity still,
to exclaim the fingers away,
with the hard, hissing
inbreath,
why would you invoke
such promises,
in every language
but the truth?

I am a believer
in many things,

but less one,
and you are straining
the good will
of the triexta. ♦

You Are The Accused

I too oft
gave voice
to the treasons
of the soul,
a calling card of a thief,
but I am stealing valor,
shadows yawning wide, set
to swallow the sfumato,
hawking mystery,
a process of becoming
unmade,
is still a process
of becoming.

The jury all
cut their names,

in that cheap
nameplate bronze,
by their mean professing –
unfounded
and further ungrounded,
though it was.

You are not the judge,
you are the accused. ♦

Requirement Of Innocence

(Berlin Oct 22)

If I should not
prevaricate each rune,
then strike them
from the eyes,
and reach,
of all us
unripe children.

Why should I attempt
the reclaiming,
of how bright
once I spoke,
or coarsen
for future's sorrow,

when it seems I really can,
promise you everything
but tomorrow.

The innocence you lose,
you never again
regain,
but you require me
less. ✦

Kitchen Session

I loved the hell
right out of you,
there lies yon
spot on cherry drop-leaf,
to this day,
to tell all:
the period blood
seeping the wood,
combing out the rug,
but not where
the fork and
knife did lay,
yea,
I loved the hell
right out of you,
and now,

I want to
give you the hell
right back. ♦

Poor William

Fever trials find me not unwilling,
if they can trace my rebellion,
they'll cut it out,
I have reason to believe
the better part of me
lies down invisible,

but live your life in earnest,
even if in anguish,

though it be temporary,
do you not
love the song
of the whip-poor-will? ◆

Remembering To Smile

Exiled of your polarity,
I am drawn neither
toward,
or away,
balancing the shove
and yank,
with nothing like a struggle,
these days,
heaped on days,
as one striving with the current,
only achieving the stream,
you can't see it from
Christendom,
Indiana,
but the interior has not
only been rearranged,

but altogether,
removed.

Remembering to smile,
and where to stow the smile,
when it fades. ◆

I am the ape
of these drained bare
streets, long past defilement-
they contain me much
less,
than I am
contained.
I am throwing everything
into the gale,
and behold,
how the gale does take me,
there is naught,
then there is
the elevator pitch.

My head
ache tells not,
my stories.

Deliver me back,
it hardly matters
where,
just back
(...just deliver). ♦

pt. II

shapeshifters

Your Wilds

(Rose Ave Los Angeles Mar 20)

Here lies another reckless domain
of hounds,
I wear them upon me
in the would-be
stillness of the bewitching hour,
under a shackled Milk Moon,
and retreating stars.
Let the windows be fastened open,
yes, I am permitting the
moribund singsong,
perking for the melody,
as ever,

cursing the cost
of living,
shorting my mail order
vindication,

and I make good on the
promise of a doomed man-
doomed to caress your face,
in the rue shadow
of every other face.

I was barely lost to your wilds,
if I sojourned there,
too great a length. ♦

(Rubies+Diamonds Los Angeles Mar 20 for Crys)

You, being bound,
to a chrysanthemum
in its bloom,
did so utilize the
escape route
through the
screened-in
porch,
you reap
three or four
words,
gliding nigh unseen, past
the cotillion armada
of easy dismantled matrons,
with their lemon wheels
and frosted sun tea,

and reckon you
know the score,

years later,
at Rubies+Diamonds
on Sunset,
you sit there and take it–
the full measure of her testimony,
and that collusive sun,
burning
spot right on,
for effect,

where was that damn sun
in December,
in the City of Dawn?

She has always just
wanted to know,

if you are hot,
or if you are cold,

and you,
have never known. ♦

The Worst Ill

Juniper subjugation...whew,
it happened to
this gun shy
cameraman,
wait, no,
the other guy,
the camera shy
gunman,
well, either way,
he dreamed he lost
the lobe of one ear,
and when he awoke,
he had forgotten how
to speak Spanish!

When it happened to me,
it was worse:
I forgot to kiss you,
when I left the house
that morning,
you know the one... ♦

Three Tongues Winking Broad

(Metronom Köln Jul 23)

I am the night's favorite excuse,
she meets me in Cologne,
and I find my spear.
Afterward,
I attempt to talk,
she well attends.
She could go on
'til 4 ay em's algid light,
all launch-ready
'to kill, feed, mate,
stopping only to
...croon,
but she speaks beyond
elegance,
with all three tongues winking broad,

I am so rapidly
a rudderless skull.
She humors me,
because she loves
her baby bird.
And I am a good sunshine,
I hold on to her
anywhere.
Let me lick you apart,
before I cave you. ♦

(Roan Mt Jul 22)

Yes, I've been through Unicoi,
and clamored for no one
in Asheville Town,
do you suppose I never saw
the sad irony in my own
enchanted myopathy,
of course,
but I knew biblically
the beauty giving way
to the mundane,
and the disappointment
in the abject lack
of appointment,
entering twined
into a litany of false hopes,

a hush born cycle of tawdry glee,
spanning to, and through,
yet another round of princely pity,

pulling the flame from the air,
and then the smoke from the flame. ♦

I In Green

Would that lola's cooking
was enough, to
salvage me and you
as us,
to convince you,
of what I in green could not,
but the host of spirits
send their regards,
from a place too far off,
a place you have either,
allowing yourself,
forgot,
or, that you have never known.

I can see all of
one side of your face,

in the mirror,
but you had
a brilliant crown of emeralds,
for the photographs,
and you knew many of the names,
for the outmost stars- and the cats
trusted you,
but they were not
your cats. ♦

Silent Game

(Henry Turner Jr's Baton Rouge Mar 21)

You are welcome
to this lovelorn congress
of chaoses,
like every newborn,
I started playing
The Silent Game,
oh, around Louisiana,
but I didn't stop
until I turned
thirty-three,
oh, sure, I had something
to say,
every now
&
every again,

but the words being
still under
contract,
I lost them
immediately,
upon contact.

Here I always meant to tell you,
about sleepwalking
through Jackson Square. ◆

One Tennessean To Another

(Overton Park Memphis Oct 20)

The gift
shop calls
forth, and
pink proves
still
dangerous,
yet, I can find
hardly a reason,
to cross the river.
I bemoan the flecks
of gold,
in the eyes of
all undressed
salamanders,

this was not
how she always
meant to die.

And shall I
never know each edge
of our sun,
again?

You who were born savior
to a better world. ♦

(Capitol D.C. Sep 19)

Trading a mother's toy town
for the capital,
the first winter,
was hard to my bones,
and every other,
though it would bestow me spring,
thus,
I availed myself
of the cherry
blossoms,
it was the only beauty
I could afford,

until I met
you. ♦

Dance Or Fight

You never have
claimed your country,
so you have seen
your diaspora
become your shell game,
is this why no one
understands you,
when you profess?
That I played gun dog
to your barren gangland soiree,
the fault is not all mine,
I followed my ancestors
up and down your spine,
unsure whether to dance
or fight,

and I spent my share,
shaking off the double takes,
I ran,
in the rain
simply to get home,
or closer anyway
-hardly pride. ♦

Sing Then Of Ashes

(Witch Creek Fire Cuyamaca Feb 23)

Ringing for the dusk,
ready to hunt,
you do not make room
for me, none do
anymore,
I have become small enough
to become unmemorable, though,
we could have once been lovers
in arms,
who will charge the town of my birth,
with its own demise?
When I quit claiming this land,
with its sky overhead,
they could finally quit
claiming me back,

I am disappearing in the mind
and memory
of the manzanitas.

Sing now of fire,
sing then of ashes. ♦

I still remember who took that photo,
they are invisible,
but there is the shadow
of their finger,
I remember where it was,
it was how she always had her hand up,
it's one way to really know someone...

a picture is just a picture. ♦

Able children of morn,

rise,

to greet a story told throughout this,

all of time,

and hesitate only as little

as you may bear,

then,

pour forth that which was first poured

into you,

you are the only shape that:

Space

Beauty,

Gravity,

and God

may take,

so,

be taken

and exalt. ♦

Symposium Of Daffodils

(Dalkey Coliemore)

I will be staying,
longer than expected,
if you ask the symposium of
daffodils,
this is already the case,
I will come to know the children,
of my words,
I have heralded their ingress,
and one day henceforth,
they will possess their own manner,
of anointing,
I am still an offering to time,
and I will have my pastures of rest,

I who have loved the sea,
and the mountain,
but most of all,
seeing one,
from the other. ◆

pt. III

eyelid removal

Deserter's Lament

(D.C. Sep 19)

I am no longer a foot soldier
in any lost cause,
I simply walked away,
from the field one day,
letting the blade become inert
at the base of a falling down wall,
taking only an illustration
of my mother
in her youth,
abandoning even my boots.
They could take me no further.

Eventually, I reached a green country,
beside a sea-like-lake,
no visible shore beyond,

and there I began to count

the sunrises,

and sunsets,

the stars blinking

on,

and off,

I never heard from my boots again. ♦

Music In The Wind

(Roanoke Jul 24)

I am happy cuz
though,
I am a mongrel,
we gave the world to one another,
and god gave it to us,
now I listen to the wind,
moving about every
thing,
(but it is not for sale)-

I know the wind in the music,
and the music
in the wind.

I was planting,
seeds,
in a dream,

since I was waiting,
for information. ♦

Every Spirit Is Sacred

(Råvarene Bergen Dec 23)

Now I return to the mountains,
rising in waves from the North
Sea, my young shall have
my world, in truth,
she was never mine,
I was born, rather,
already half ghost
to the slate dusk emergent,
I suffered my youth
the most,
but as a bulwark
of a man, I like my body,
thick and full,
the additional air it consumes,
to charge,

the summit is finally my
mother father,
I traverse easily
these depths,
here,
every spirit
is sacred.

Even the light whispers to the dawn. ♦

Ask My Desert, Ask The Sun

(Turtle Rock Joshua Tree Nov 19)

Sharing the desert

with the sun,

I am not learning,

or trying,

to sing clearer,

but I have fallen to

hearing beneath

the silence,

the song in all,

whether you listen,

or hear,

or no,

and stars behind the stars,

just ask my desert, ask the sun. ♦

Saint Mark's stitched me up
but good,
and that cuts
both ways,
please, do not speak to me
of beauty,
coarse or otherwise,
not here,
gross provisions
of any value,
I left behind,
in the town
of Independence,
that is,
I gave away
the ending,
and quick ran
out of dead marsh land

in which to return things,

unto the earth,

so I let some perish,

under the eyes,

of the sun,

enlisting the aid of

others,

cast off characters,

whose hands were full

of fists,

from the first,

they did my discarding,

too gladly,

and I lose the porcelain twice. ♦

All Across Of A Midnight

(Hotel Schweizerhof Bern Feb 24)

I can scarce afford
my unminted saints
these days,
I held a miracle once,
for a moment,
but not when I needed it most,
this is not (yet) a dissertation
on the generosity of lovers,
though, hardly the laundry list
of complaints I let fly against
the barricades of conceit,
do not spend your small,
paltry grace of time,
in idle talk,

rather,

idle dancing,

all across of a midnight.

I said my peace,

if only to the memory

of stars. ◆

(Barcelona Mar 23)

I let go of you the very moment
I no longer hold on
to anything,
if everyone in
Plaça del Sol
is falling together
through space,
am I no longer part,
of everyone?
If ever I was,
I found succor in the language
of my own provenance
and banishment,
so be it,
I lost,
and left,
salvation there,

also the same place
of proud reckoning,
that providence foretells,

did you know that,
like the ruby-
tail,
I feed a thousand
times,
every
day? ♦

Just Start Moving

Your body remembers,
the way,
even if your spirit,
lies dismantled,
strewn across so many
unreachable places.

Through moving,
you will gather each fragment.
You will lean down,
kneeling,
often prostrating,
and you will pick up
the tattered remains -
torn back,

as they were once
torn away.

You may someday,
learn to marvel,
the short, sharp intakes
of breath,
replaced slowly,
by a whistling out,
catching the air between
your breath,
just so.

And you begin to find,
yourself even wondering,
at each jagged piece,
glistening there,
catching the light

amidst the dust,
and shadow,
beginning to see how
they, of all shapes and sizes,
could fit together:
before,
and perhaps after.

But the picture is either
forgotten,
or completely new.

Just start moving. ♦

Forgetting How To See

Force-feed me back what I knew
in adolescence,
bring the spoon
and the ladder
brigade,
if you think that'll help,
rather than castrate the final
scope of ignorance,
that hovers near,
ever over one shoulder,
we,
being each brought to this world,
cold,
hungry,
and alone,
this is also how we leave.

The moments between,
this is when we learn
how to look,
before forgetting,
how to see. ♦

Behind Us Dark

(for LCNF)

All that bears my name,
slowly fading into
behind us dark,
we cannot see
it occur,
since it does not occur
at once,
but we sing
together by the absence,
though only when
we have noticed
it is missing,
and late is the time,
to hold it back.

You are proof that
I exist. ♦

Either way,
I'll sleep better tonight,
you would not even believe
what plagues me now,
for once I understand
how cologne can smell
"cheap",
I wore it too,
once,
now it wears me
out,
you can be as refined
and mighty
as the bender will allow,
I will merely sit
downstream,
and allow myself
to forget the tingling

in the skin
of my skull,
full of these discount
surprises.

I look forward,
to
sleeping,
with the blinds unclosed,
with you. ♦

Good Dancers

Hail the universal beauty queen,
bet that dog knows deep joy,
while I am using my luck
to survive,
I will not burden you now,
with the task of remembering,
merely,
let it be known I have been forsaken
by the gods,
all of them...
movin' up in the world,
well,
at least
movin' 'round,
and all good dancers
fall. ♦

You should have seen me,
with my petals,
in my blush,
I never considered how
the light did constantly
change,
I did not count the rain,
I became obsessed with
burning down the artifice,
of my fabled origins,
even while chanting the same,
to my masses,
I was as negligent,
as I have maintained,
still beyond the scope,
of any industry,
my integrity,
in its frame of inchoate abdication,
as ever, walked before me,

word gets around,

such is the blister of

every homespun glory,

I am acquainted with your ceiling,

ever since it became our floor,

I'd kill

for a cup,

of cool water,

or, for any other reason. ♦

(Kadıköy Istanbul Mar 24)

They got me with the floor plan,
and the lighting,
but such is the layout
of the proletariat
and modern mercenary,
let posterity
sift and sort,
rather,
do the math,
zero is less than a number,
try and explain
it to anyone
but my nephew,
we who teach by parable,
packed up for Constantinople
and a nose job,
the hashish guides my sword,

I do not need you to understand,
understand? ♦

VOLUME II:
INSIDE THE BODY IS DARK

pt. IV

mourn tiger

Always so much on the line,
that the tiny scrapes
around the edges,
get surrendered,
then abandoned,
it's why they were painted in
at all,
and you intimately
do not feel,
the loss of them,
focused as you are,
on not
losing too much more. ♦

Hardly Worthy

You never met the organist,
well, I did,
and I remember those gusset shoes,
and that she dimmed the lights
to off,
before we began,
and drew her breath,
to draw down
those aching accordion
blinds,
when it was all over,
as her husband watched,
through the hidden camera,
while eating a salted kiwi.

No music
(though she truly played
with,
and from the heart),
can hold it all back,
or all together,
and the shoes
had their own secrets obviously...

we make ourselves so pretty,
and it is hardly worthy of its noise. ♦

Forget it, Armstrong,
you are not to be
the caretaker of
another distended reality,
and no misplaced bravado
will bring the
doves back
to the woods,

I say,
let the dogs
have at the body
first for
once-

you,
ever the son of
a banker,

surely,

you count the cost,

of proving right,

the hunter's firstborn. ♦

Wanderlust Companion

(Shakey's Asheville Aug 22)

From sharp to souring,
glistens the refrain,
she would let the cheap
wine breathe,
you didn't pay
attention,
as you should,
so you haunt the
dividends,
you can ask too many
questions though,
or not enough,
actually, I'm fine,
you just need to know
where to look,

in shorter than the time
it takes to turn,
and check the door lock,
but this door doesn't,
only rattles,
then, you and your latest
wanderlust companion,
fall to relying on twiddling the point,
of the pocketknife,
laughing the grim
fiasco of the latest shift
in local gravity,
don't keep the limbo to yourselves,
adept you have no right
to avow,
but,
haven't you noticed, how
the light has gone? ♦

Aw Men

My solemn teacher's bleak aphorism,
still beating the dreck,
was cardiovascular,
and perfectly attuned to
the long range
vacuum waves,
spurting out of
the wrong end of
the present tense,
and straight into
the gaping mouth,
of her
tailpipe.

She was rubber where
it counted,

and steel
everywhere else,
with all her power
and glory,

ah-men. ♦

Meadow Queen

(Julian for JS)

The honor of only tragedy,
found Mildred,
that night on the parade
float,
by cover of darkness-
little Millie,
meadow queen,
and freckle
face...

never caught 'em,
never will,
we will,
will it away,

and she won't,
wear those braids again,

they broke her,
that night,
spit-roasted her all the way in half,
and no one
could bring her back,

no doctor,
no lover,
and no mother.

She still smiles,
pretty fair,
though,
as I have always held. ♦

Upend September

(Ballard SS Dec 23)

Yum & coke,
I really didn't plan on
drinking tonight,
he from Chiang Mai
talkin' 'bout,
buying mushrooms,
she talking
chant'relles,
no one can agree,
upend September,
and the leading man,
plays it kinda like,
he is not,
the leading man,
which kinda sells it-

it's not even necessarily about

the hair-

the dusky close-out dilemma,

as the same song keeps jumping

on the juke,

every so often too often,

you understand pretty well,

why,

when the glass is full

to brimming,

it will be fuller still,

once the ice softens,

and watch how it just becomes

dismal,

saltwater,

time to go! ♦

Me & Dimitri

(Rose Ave Venice Apr 20)

ELL EYY,
and here you thought
it was pronounced,
"laaa"
as far a place,
and as good a one to die,
still with the wasteland ego,
and they have it
in my size,
I brought my respirator along,
simply to get a table,
the band was on late,
but I wasn't on Atlanta
time no more,

the way the clocks
had all been synchronized
to be disabled,
at the same time,
Dimitri kicks
me full
in the teeth,
right as I was grand
standing
my first exposure,
it's a right mess
of freeform
incisors
and K-9s,
there I am,
shaking the life
out of all hands offered,
but with the wrong hand,

and looking away,
not at anything particular,
you can see the transfiguration
taking its rightful place,
in the orchestra section,
amidst the purfled dahlias
in my eyes:
open,
but flying to wild,
but then I see you.

And someone starts the clock again. ◆

Two-Handed Saw

Father was a brisk cutter,
with the two-handed
saw,
the cold demanded
the quick time,
I was raised
by the fire,
prone upon
the hearth,
hearing the flames,
whisper
to the stones,
and beyond,
always the wind,
whipping the air,
drawing our breath away,

even as she
would push the blaze,
to blacken. ♦

The Time Of Manu

You are a lion's share,
and I am
that cat.

Awaken to thy glory,
oh my heart,
today we shall not,
give the gods
their fire back.

It is my time,
the time of Manu. ♦

Oh ye host of closet mystics,
even the debutante class,
with its right
to grease,
has its myriad processionals,
paying the ferry toll,
knifing the eyes,
with plastic
punch-out
spoons,
scrape all you want,
at the headboard,
my lovely dust heads,
stalking empty
Barna,
you may seize
all you want,

there is always
a li'l more,
riding
along the infinite,
reparations of remorse. ♦

7 Second Delay

And did you know,
your face
was ever so briefly
shown,
on-screen,
for 3.5 seconds,
impregnable,
and hardest to place
-a tourist
with a costume,
for every day of the week-
during the Open,
blurred behind above,
the second seed,

the prime-time
slo-mo
close-up,
telling it like it
was,
camera #2 looking
for a reaction,
not discovering your arc light,
coiling under wraps,
and cover of night,
as few have cared to do,
before languidly,
panning left,
up, and away,
the 7 second delay
not wasting its breath,
cutting to the watch commercial
(that'd been watched
already too many times),

it happened,
as I happened
to look down,
maybe around

(something in my lap,
perhaps,
a light fizzling out,
in the hall,
buzzing in the kitchen,
appliances turning themselves on,
turning themselves off),

but it is enough
to know,
such things
are not impossible,

officially,

my response

to all you represent,

has hobbled magnificently

heavenward,

but

in texture,

hardly tone-

I would, to this day,

not give

ground on you,

and rely,

on the way you have always smelled,

though it was a career performance,

everyone said so,

4 grueling hours,

and 3 minutes more,

the exact length
of time
(and occurring at exactly the same
time),
907 miles south,
my brother drags his car
out of the ditch,
how is your brother,
by the way?
He and I got on
something like fine,
ever since
he smacked his head,
on the wake,
our first summer-
came up gasping,
grasping for my hand,
dragged him out of the lake,
called your father,

swing too hard,
you're gonna swing loose,
I might have said,
I might say so,
now,

I'm not certain
when I became,
that friend
with the sports news
networks,
in tow,

but I became
many things,
by addition,
and subtraction,

give me 1 good reason,
why I would still
look for your face,
in a place like this?

And no,
the kids don't count. ✦

King At A Run

(to JI)

You are the king,
at a run,
but when you forget
to dance, you forego
the need
of interludes,
and time passes
unpleasantly,
in that disturbing fashion
where, between the nodules
striking out the riverbed,
some plentiful eyelids,
stuck apart,

a coming to,
on either side,
of this or that dead crosswalk,
the unflinching intervals,
of unrented patio
fixtures,
damn,
burn me alive for once.

I would start walking. ♦

pt. V

inquisitional soma

Dispensation Of Benedictions

To be pardoned on merit,
and merit alone,
leave the swoop,
of my thighs,
out of the running,
may I now return,
every kiss I stole in my mouth,
in my youth?
They have long
plagued the parched
cinderblocks,
I had to remove
myself to the attic,
to maintain
any sort of view,

I have no power
to cast the curses anymore,
but I retain
the same enough
dispensation
of benedictions. ♦

(Kalogeros Paros Mar 24)

I can't picture you much other,
than you already are,
but I had to learn,
to accept,
I would never know the silent
part of you,
though it rules you hard over,
if I could but reach,
slightly more under,
the skin, I would
have hold of you –
but my hands
are either too big,
or too slow,
to get in,
and then,
back out. ◆

Lost My Birds

(Stockholm Oct 21)

I am last to admit
summer has ended,
I reckon I exist as much
to every remnant
recollection,
as to what I will still owe
tomorrow,
it is a fine thing,
only,
to have been...

though I may
see it different,
come November,

I am yet
bone augurer,
since I lost
my birds. ♦

Take Or Take Leave

Who laughs at ya in Newcastle,
they'd have to laugh
at themselves,
it's for the merchants,
and the cold,
it's for the laden dram
of certitude,
and then forgetting
where ya came from,
though you never
leave,
let your blossoms bloom
in full,
entombed,
some scarce, noble eve,
say,

October, weeks in,
with the chill,
that hardly forsook,
and allow a foreigner
to pluck ya,
and fuck propriety,
which is what you suckle,
and he can take,
or take leave. ♦

Filling space,

is one rationale,

for space,

but so is,

clearing all,

to create,

space,

we are as much empty,

as not,

flowing broad,

through,

not around -

remember that,

next time you open,

your mouth. ♦

One Of Your
Discarded Evenings

Following the curves,
which are curving to be
followed,
forgetting I was
far from anything anyone would call
home,
but fixing my hair nonetheless,
as well as the quivering reflection
would portray,
I came to a better Prague,
signing out my last resolve,
as a tattered charm
of relinquishment,
for the night,

becoming more

my marionette,

and drudging up,

to dance,

my brave bitter retreat,

into an indentured conclave,

and a plague on lesser shadows,

but for candlelight,

I would hope to patter

by presumption,

a sanction on disbelief,

I spent everything I had,

after selling everything I own,

just to stand on the corner,

and discover a bygone myth

of tomorrow,

in one of your discarded evenings. ♦

Exaggerated Cinnabar

(LHR-CDG Aug 15)

It's not easy to request a murderer,
watching the interstitial tango
of two Phalènes,
who, meet for the first time,
where, the square is bookended by
children's carnivals,
the real neighborhood shuttered,
or, just packing it away,
such are the thoughts of a cloud
of December,
approaching the mountains,
the dilemma,
if you continue stroking it upon
exaggerated cinnabar as such,

is that every gaze, gesture,
and grafting exchange,
sticks hard to its oblivion
prescription,
before you arrive mise en scène-

this is where the murder plot
draws blood,
splashing the backdrop. ♦

The Magnetism Of Dust

This is not a prophet's party,
I don't know why I stayed,
the wine flows freely enough,
but there used to be
more shades of amber
and easy laughter,

my heart still seasonally dwells
in Grenada,
and receives the island of your love's
blood,
thriving on the manioc
and sugarcane,

I came calling,
upon a reminiscence,

as it wavered near
its event horizon,
scheduled for deletion,
on the grounds of wilting
to nothing,

and I could have told myself
anything,
instead,
I watched from a distance too great
to hear anything clear,
feeling the pulse and pierce
all over again...
I forgot about that shirt,
those shoes,
and that supercilious
chagrin,

you did not write the dialogue
of our reckoning,
and you cannot dictate
its demise,
you are, after all,
peering through
your pet stigmatism,
preoccupied with
what your hands are doing,
recording the motion
of your feet,
letting the words falter
fast and apart,
to the bastion of each
surpassing moment,
though can you say where one ends,
and the next begins,
ever intending to bind each
together,

to abide time,
with the unguent of your self,
and whatever is lying about
within your satchel of
what collects around you,
through the magnetism
of dust,
or through adherence by survival,
precious, though light,
all of which will manage
to show you
both faithless,
and dear,

you carried the only urgency,
all the while,
and much is made of the will,

and to think,
the flowers never need
make answer,

your favorite pastime to be,
will become,
making predictions-
read the room. ♦

Humorless child...yes,
I've known a few,
(I knew myself then),
I showed them where to rest,
and water the ponies,
but as a bystander,
innocent, or perhaps
otherwise,
I still regret,
the tenement fire I gave out on,
was only a hired facade,
and when they screamed "cut!"
I was actually surprised,
they scorned me
by blessing me, but I was born
used to just such, or,
such just treatment,
and I scrap when I'm bored,
not indignant.

When I asked if she knew,

she was a character in my dream,

she responded,

by asking,

if I knew,

that she,

was,

the dream. ♦

Cherub Tormentor

(Montreal Margot)

A trifling morsel of personal evil,
gone to code,
let it have its day,
and give me back
my left shoe,
I need it to leave,
this, and all such places,
and I can't stay,
and you won't ask-
some frantic shuffling
of the cues,
and I'm gone,
my shirt is on,
backwards,
but it's on.

Good
night & bye,
my cherub
tormentor,
if you truly are a sadist,
then I truly let you be. ♦

Milk Run, Supposedly

(Seaside Heights NJ May 08)

You, me- capital venturists
of a tall order,
jumping the slick seals through
the rings, I heard you were
a dock worker,
before,
staring straight down into the sea,
by which you never
left the harbor,
sure, I wanted to sit by
you, the moment I walked
in, it was the only available
chair,
and the view
was better,

than downstairs,
but it always is
invisible,
this was supposed to be
a milk run,
and now we're fixing to kill
or die,

I hate Mondays. ♦

(Prague Na skleničku for S)

Your eyes are almost too tired,
and I've got somewhere to be,
convince me in 5 seconds
or less,
otherwise,
I donned my finery
for nothing
and no one,
I like the cocktail
of you,
or something like you,
I wish
you would be more like
something I like,
I will bend,
I am willing to blend
and blur the picture,

to almost,
make you so,
you're close enough,
you're nearly there,
somewhere I can deposit my bones,
for a quick spell,

you have 2 seconds
left. ♦

Bees Of Heaven

(Homer AK for SM)

I must remember
to send the bees of heaven
to you,

for when
you reminded me
of the colors
of my wardrobe,
every spring,
in the land of hollyhocks,
and calico country,

where the sun doesn't set down,
only touches,
and goes. ◆

pt. VI

rings around the sun

Save The World Then End It

You're going back in time again,
aren't you,
since, you can no longer
travel,
any other way,
do we know each other,
there?
And do you seek to save the world,
then end it?

I will need to travel too,
but a different way,
to remember –
to catch up
with you
tomorrow. ♦

Now do I finally submit,
to the grand marketing scheme,
that was assigned me at birth,
the only chance I ever stood,
departed age 14, when I somehow
thought I wore a 13,
was I too alone,
or,
not isolated enough,
I learned to cook,
only to receive the masses,
and I fielded the same trouble,
I would always,
was I rushing mad down
the dirt drive,
after that ragged square of blue,
that El Niño blew
through the pass,

was the stiff clay
underfoot, my sole
inheritance,
merely running away
beneath me,

if I thought overmuch
of human love,
it was only to account,
in measure,
the less she thought of me,

the hills were my first home,
and I have been returning
from the holy land,
ever since. ✦

I Mainly Squander Daylight

(Au Pied de Cochon Paris Mar 23)

A silver nautilus retrospective,
and a token shimmer of cold
gold, in this otherwise monochrome
puppet show in reverse,
Paris, Tennessee in the rain,
blacktop still wearing its venerable
veil of silence,
I did not know I was giving away
so much
of the furniture
in that moment,
but god I hope they'll let me keep
my lease,
so many uncertain conditions abroad,

you are liable

to proclaim,

to have failed the fine print,

especially,

if you attempt to flee,

the won't let you back

in to Paradise,

for example,

when once they handed you the keys

to the city,

but it is for the best,

I guess,

since I mainly squander daylight. ⬧

Neither Of These

The tabloid of the bricks
sells its story
to the morning commute,
but it's not the overture
I once tallied and trusted,
the heart surgery
left me heartless,
then I decided
every other Thursday
I wouldn't open my mouth,
by order of
the lower intestine,
it is to be my introduction,
to the twin I never knew
I had,
who died there

in the dark,
before being born.

If there is only one who may
proffer the invitation,
and only one to whom
it may be proffered,
I am neither,
of these. ♦

(Norbergsgatan 24)

So it is,
your dreams are coming true.

True, the dreams had to change,
radically
and remorselessly,
but largely,
glad you are,
that they could,
you concede now,
why your ancestor kept his omens
close,
but vague,
what did he name Long Island,
it may be too late to ask,
but not too late
to really care,

144

time will take of us all,
but this one moment, at least,
is not spoken for,
and belongs wholly
to you,

you cannot keep it,
only shear one lock of pure gold,
so it may outlive you,
and secure it where you hold
all sacred things,
sacred and terrible. ◆

Any Every

(Malmö)

These days, it could be any you,
looking down into the street,
from any window...
are you two candles, one askew,
or perhaps,
terrier longingly behind
widow's thrill...

I know how you move
and moan,
in your sleep, but
I don't know why,
I almost lost you in Bristol
before we ever began,

146

I blamed the rain, and
the traffic, the heat,
...my fickle heart,

the last thing I could see,
you were amongst your rage,
before retreating back
to your flat,

with its one window,
looking down
into every street. ♦

(Leidseplein Jul 3)

If ever I become a gentle savage,
do me the courtesy
of chucking me down the well,
I have seen every sun rising
at midnight,
but thought not
of tomorrow,
as every pebble knows it is sand,
do you?

You attain not to the glory
of a second glance,
better to come to know
solitude in the utmost,
then at least,
you will still be known,
to your voids,

148

do not give away the only thing
you have to give,
nothingness becomes the night,
but you wake with the dawn. ♦

In All Her Corners

(BNA-JFK-BOM)

What will we speak of
when we are older?

Perhaps a kingdom
of many bright lanterns
I saw from the railing,
and other places
gilded, gleaming in the mist,

how I arrived by boat,
and you,
by a whisper,

your mother is more than her bones -
you and I may realize this,
in the same moment,

I was the quiet one,
in all her corners,
an exile,
yet a baron,

ever wandering not in asperity,
for I have loved every fabrication
where people may live,

and how can I show you all I know,
and only what you can taste. ♦

The Beauty
Of My Eye's
Beholding

(Soho Grand Nov 19)

Some may say,
I gave my breath away
too easy,
I held such small sway
over anything but my limbs,
I listen back to my reflections,
and quickly improvise
a numeric admonition,
to whisper the distance,
and difference,
between them,
though I am a drifter,
I have come to love my bearings,

and the beauty of my eye's beholding,

suffers, and dies with me,

please inter,

my sundry selves,

alongside,

which did so resonate,

with each frequency,

of handheld stars. ♦

When I had a reputation,
it was hardly bronze,
I let the reins go,
a bump in the road fetched them,
back up to me,
but my, how the miles had drifted,
and dusted,
I'll give you one shot for free,
said she,
but it wasn't my best,
and I've been aiming into,
and at,
the dark,
ever since.
I knew for whom,
they dug that bed of earth,
and I smelled them cutting pine,
let me tell you how I drove
the ox cart south,

following a trail of black birds,
when I reached the gulf,
I turned the timbers sideways,
and house-shaped,

you already know
how I won your heart,
in a game of chance. ♦

Celandines

(Strand Hamburg)

Berlin by morning,
as a star is birthed in the belly,
of my beloved beast,
a sonnet and an ode,
for the sesame seed,
that is my fledgling world,
whatever you say next,
will come to pass,
so,
tell any story you like,
as long as you are a subject,
of gravity,
and grace,
I wish you not unremittingly,
hurt,

but I know joy,
will find you,
my mother was even known
to smile,
for the camera,
and I followed that whim
through the ages,
and now, it possesses the power,
to weep and bleed from
every chorus line,
if I was hardened in my spirit
until I became see through,
at least I chose when to care,
even as my cares chose me
as bearer,

I regularly commune with
the monarch of death,
but also the jaunt of rebirth,

therefore, I merely
commune,
and watch meat fly
through space,
in the guise of any average angel,
not a prayer nor a curse
upon the lips,
but the wind ever beneath
the wings.

If ever I bring you to Berlin,
remind me to tell you
of the celandines. ♦

Don't miss this,
be unto every part of it,
if you will only see,
once,
be sure to be seen
there,
your eyes clear,
and fully wide.

Drink of the wedding wine,
and make peace,
finally,
with the warring years,
stretching behind you,
but unable,
to stretch any further
beyond you. ♦

I will plant in the spring,
if a young god still favors
my breath,
and if the weight of the wind,
is still the lighter for it,
the days of drinking mead
are through,
and the love I had
for my pipe and my fur,
cast off,
in almost disdain,
for I was born in my skin,
and I think I'll live in it too.

We never intend to die,
though we intend to know
we must,
and if I live to see spring,
let autumn be as yet unpromised. ♦

END